NOR

CW01456732

MYTHOLOGY

Tales of Nordic Gods, Heroes, Yggdrasil, Norse Magic & Viking Lore.

CONTENTS

INTRODUCTION

V ikings are often depicted as fierce warriors who raided and plundered coastal towns in the 8th century Europe. But as celebrated historians such as Philip Parker and Fenella Bazin describe, the Viking world had a rich culture that influenced our modern surroundings.

The first recorded account of a Viking raid happened in 793 A.D. when armed warriors attacked the monastery of Lindisfarne located on the coast of Northumbria - an early kingdom in England. The monks were defenseless as the raiders plundered the edifice to steal gold, food, and captives. It was the first in the series of raids conducted by Scandinavian pirates who would continue to attack coastal towns in Europe for the next two centuries.

Vikings are portrayed as ferocious warriors by early chroniclers who experienced the raids. However, all of the historians of that age were Christians who demonized the Viking warriors in their accounts. For example, Abbot Alcuin of York dramatically recorded the Lindisfarne raid. He wrote "the church was splattered with the blood of priests of God, despoiled of all its ornaments...given as a prey to pagans."

But despite their violent and destructive attacks, the Vikings played a crucial role in the vastness of the Scandinavian world. Aside from raiding towns, they were also excellent traders who even reached Russia to barter goods. They were pioneers in sea exploration sending long ships to navigate the Atlantic to even land in North America centuries before Christopher Columbus. They were artists who created sophisticated works of art and poets who composed prose sagas and verses about great stories that we can still hear today.

In this book, we will explore the rich and vivid world of the Vikings - their origins, myths, pantheon, beliefs, magical practices, and their influence on our modern society.

CHAPTER ONE

VIKING ORIGINS

Modern-day Sweden, Norway, and Denmark were home to the Vikings before they became unified countries. The Viking homeland was predominantly rural with no central settlements. Not all Vikings were warriors or raiders, as a majority of the population earned their keep through fishing or through agriculture.

Historians agree that the term Viking originated from the Scandinavian word *vikingr* which means pirate. The word is generally used to refer to sea voyages, and was mainly used by Scandinavians as a verb to refer to men who take their time to go "viking". The word functions pretty much the same as our modern-day skiing during winter. Furthermore, these sea expeditions are not all about raiding coastal towns as many of them are destined for overseas trade.

However, it is interesting to take note that early records do not refer to these seaborne raiders as Vikings, appearing commonly in the 11th century. Instead, early defenders use different names to refer to them – Normanni (Northmen), Pagani (Pagans), or Dani (Danes).

Viking Raids in England

After the famous attack at the monastery of Lindisfarne, other monasteries, coastal villages, and even large cities in Europe found themselves besieged by these foreign raiders. Because of the increasing frequency of sea attacks, defending villages learned new ways to deter raids such as sea-facing stone walls, walled-in harbors, stone high towers, and archery fortification.

The purpose of these attacks are not yet clear and it is even part of debate among historians. One popular theory is that Vikings had to escape the harsh climate of the North. But this is still not yet definitive as they still return to their homeland with treasures and captives to survive the harsh winter ahead. Vikings may have learned from traders and merchants about the riches on the western settlements. After the attack in St. Cuthbert, Vikings attacked Scotland in 794, Ireland in 795, and France in 799.

The initial raids were small mainly composed of few boats and warriors who would immediately return to their homeland once they have plundered enough treasure or captives, or if the defenders were too strong and able to hold them off. But after a few years, they started to rally longer attacks in France, Ireland, and England where they established their foundations and started dominating inland areas.

The attacks reached a peak during the second half of the 9th century. In Orkneys, Scotland, the Vikings even established an earldom and invaded Hebrides and Shetlands.

In France, the Vikings quickly framed its dominion as the Frankish kingdom of that time was tainted by political instability. In fact, Paris was besieged and almost captured by a Viking Army in 885. Meanwhile in Ireland, the Vikings built fortified ports that served as their garrison for dominating the eastern region of the island.

A massive Viking army arrived in England in 865. The army was led by warrior siblings Ivar and Halfdan who conquered several kingdoms in Anglo-Saxon England. The first kingdom they captured was Northumbria in 866, they later conquered East Anglia, then Mercia - the central kingdom of that time. The kingdom of Wessex was the only dominion not invaded by the Vikings.

King Alfred was nearly defeated by the Vikings, but still won the significant Edington battle of 879. He successfully managed to keep Viking threats at bay by reorganizing the military service and effective use of garrisoned fortresses around Wessex. Hence, King Alfred played a major role in the English History as the defender of the Christian faith against Viking pagans. Because of his great accomplishments, he was later called Alfred the Great.

For almost a century, England was divided between the land dominated by Wessex kings in the south and colonies controlled by Vikings in the north and midlands. The last Viking king who hold over the English soil was Erik Bloodaxe who was expelled by Wessex in 954.

Vikings still controlled major regions in Scotland, a small area in France and Dublin in Ireland. In Normandy, King Charles the Simple granted land to Rollo a Norwegian Chieftain who was the great great grandfather of William the Conqueror.

Despite their expulsion from England the Vikings still controlled large parts of Russia and Ukraine where they even established their roots in Kiev and Novgorod.

Other Viking Settlements

Unlike their first attacks where they sail home after plundering enough treasures, the succeeding attacks were primarily missions of conquest. The Vikings discovered that the weather and soil was much better in England than in Scandinavia. Hence, once the army attacked a British settlement, they would send for their families to become farmers in England.

There is no unifying reason why Vikings sailed across the globe and establishing new settlements. The motivations are varied as are the men who undertook these voyages. Some desiring the treasures and riches from new lands, some chasing honor and prestige, and others wish to be in the vision of their gods and will be rewarded in the after life.

Vikings were also driven by personal freedom, political ambition, control of trade, desire for wealth, and legacy. Below are major regions across the globe where Vikings established their settlements:

The Faroe Islands

The Vikings reach the uninhabited Faroe Islands during their western expansion. The islands are located around halfway between eastern Iceland and northern Scotland. A record written in 825 by an Irish monk shows that the Island had been inhabited by monks for many years but had to depart upon the settlement of the Northmen. The Vikings called the Faroe Islands as Fareyjar or Sheep Islands. There were no trees in the islands, so the Norse settlers built their homes from rock and turf. Their livelihood was largely dependent on fishing and livestock.

Iceland

The Vikings first reached Iceland in 860. However, they were dismayed by the harsh winter, and they did not establish a settlement. In fact, the name Iceland was given by the Vikings because of the climate in the country.

The exploratory group was then succeeded by settlers after a decade, and historical records show that almost half of them that came from Norway wanted to escape the harsh regime of King Harald Fairhair.

Greenland

Based on the medieval Icelandic sagas, Erik the Red founded the Viking settlement in Greenland. Erik, noted for his fiery red hair and beard, was originally from Norway, but was outlawed "because of some killings". He named the land west of Iceland as Greenland to encourage others to join him to settle.

While Greenland's climate was colder than Iceland, there are several coastal areas that are sufficiently green for raising livestock.

In 985, 25 Viking ships left Iceland to sail for Greenland. However, only 14 made it to land as the other ships disappeared or were destroyed by the rough sea voyage. Viking settlers established farmstead in the east and west as the Inuit's lived far north during that time.

Greenland was not the best place for farming, so Viking settlers had to depend on fishing and hunting for wild sea animals such as whales, seals, and walruses. These animals were highly prized during that age, so they made a good living through trade.

Between the 15th and 17th centuries, the entire Viking population in Greenland suddenly disappeared.

Although there are different theories to explain the disappearance, no one really knows what happened.

Russia

Vikings also founded the Rurikid dynasty in Russia from the 9th to the 16th century. They were known as the Rus, in which Russia got its modern name. While the Russians are mostly Slavic, the ruling class descended from Scandinavian conquerors.

Life in the Viking Age

While the Vikings are noted for their vicious raids and plundering, most of their lives are devoted in tending to their farms and livestock. Even warriors lived on rural towns and participate in farmstead work for their subsistence and to gather supplies for winter.

Men and women have their own specific work. Women usually take care of household tasks such as preparing food and making clothes. On the other hand, men take care of tasks outside the home such as farming, fishing, or tending to the livestock. But during the harvesting period, everyone would usually join the work including children. Tasks that are physically demanding such as pulling the plow, constructing buildings, and dunging fields are delegated to slaves that were captured during raids or battles.

Other specialized crafts like ironwork are usually performed within the farmsteads and only done as needed. There are professional blacksmiths in some urban areas but they would usually ask for food or payment in exchange of their services.

Viking farm work was grueling and perilous as everything required a lot of work to achieve the basic tasks. There were no advanced tools back then to assist in the farm work. They also had to face harsh winters, and when the farmstead work has been interrupted by natural disasters, raids, or famines, many of the Viking families had no means to survive during long winters.

Diseases and famine were quite common during this era, and archaeological records show that around 30% of children died before they even reached adulthood.

Vikings mainly used horses as a primary land transport, although wagons and carts were also used to transport heavier goods. During heavy snow, skis and sleds were also crafted and implemented in day to day tasks.

Viking Social Structure

The Vikings are composed of three social classes – earls, free folks, and slaves.

The earls are on top of the social structure. They were originally warlords or chieftains who had amassed great wealth and warriors through their raiding and battles. Eventually, when the monarchy was installed in Scandinavia, the earls became aristocrats who were granted lands.

Most Vikings, even the warriors and farmers are classified as free folks. Farmers often work on their own lands, while others who don't have farms were under the employ of wealthier farmers. Other free folks were soldiers, merchants, and trades people. Basically, free men have their rights and privileges protected by the Viking law.

The warriors are mainly free men who don't have wealth or land. They choose to join the raids to acquire land or tangible rewards such as gold or silver. Many of them are not married so they are not tied down to domestic life or farm work. Viking fathers would often choose to bestow most of their wealth to their first born, so most warriors are composed of younger men who had not received substantial inheritance from their fathers.

There were three ways to become a slave in the Viking world. First was simply to be born a slave. The children of slaves were also considered as slaves. The second was to be captured in a raid or battle. The primary basis for this is the law of reciprocity, in which the Vikings believe that anyone who was captured in a war and has been spared had been provided a significant gift (his or her life) that he had to pay back with an equally significant gift (his freedom).

Bankruptcy is the third ground for slavery. The principle of reciprocity is also used in this scenario. A Viking who is extremely poor can exchange his freedom to a wealthier Viking who can take care of his material needs. This was customary for poor people who had acquired high debts, and the only way to pay his creditor is to give up his freedom.

CHAPTER TWO

THE CONCEPTION OF THE WORLD: YGGDRASIL, CREATION & THE AFTERLIFE

A t the core of the Nordic spiritual cosmology is the Yggdrasil, which is a large ash tree that grows from the *Urðarbrunnr* or the Well of Urd. Its branches held the *Niu Heimar* or the Nine Worlds, which are the realms of different beings in the Nordic Universe.

The Nine Worlds are the following:

Asgard

Asgard is the home of the Aesir, tribe of gods and goddesses. Vikings believe that this realm is located in the spiritual sky and connected to Midgard (the realm of humans) through the Bifrost, or the rainbow bridge. The suffix *-gard* in this realm's name is a reference to the Nordic concept of the difference between the *Utangard* and the *Innangard*. Utangard (beyond the fence) is wild, anarchic, and chaotic, while Innangard (inside the fence) is civilized, law-abiding, and orderly.

Asgard is considered as the best example of *Innangard*, while Jotunheim or the home of the frost giants, is the perfect example of the *Utangard*.

Midgard

Midgard or *Miðgarðr* in Old Norse is the home of the human beings. In Nordic cosmology, this is the only realm that dwells in the visible world as other realms are located in invisible locations. Its name refers to Middle Enclosure, in which it lies between the orderly realm of Asgard and the chaotic world of Jotunheim. The Vikings believed that a large serpent named Jormungand lives in the ocean and surrounds Midgard.

Vanaheim

Vanaheim or *Vanaheimr* in the Old Norse language is the home of the Vanir tribe of gods and goddesses. These deities are more associated with nature compared to the Aesir deities. Unlike Asgard and Midgard that ends with the suffix *-gard*, this realm ends in *-heim*, which means that this world is somehow natural and less civilized in comparison to Asgard.

Jotunheim

Jotunheim or *Jötunheimr* in Old Norse is the home of the giants. It is also known as Utgard or outside the fence in reference to its chaotic world. In the Poetic Eddas, Jotunheim is described as a realm that is filled with mountain peaks and dark forests where winter is never-ending.

Niflheim

Niflheim or *Niflheimr* in Old Norse is known as the primordial world of fog, ice, mist, cold, and darkness. It is the opposite realm of Muspelheim or the land of fire and heat. In the Nordic creation story, the giant Ymir was born when the fire from Muspelheim and the ice from Niflheim met in the center of

Ginnungagap, which was the fissure that had previously divided the two realms.

Muspelheim

Muspelheim or *Múspellsheimr* in Old Norse is the home of the fire giants. It is the opposite realm of Niflheim or the land of ice and mist. In the Nordic creation story, the giant Ymir was born when the fire from Muspelheim and the ice from Niflheim met in the center of Ginnungagap or the fissure that had previously divided the two realms.

Alfheim

Alfheim or *Álfheimr* in Old Norse is the realm of the elves. In Nordic mythology, elvese are demigod-like beings that are described as "luminous and more beautiful than the sun". Freyr, one of the Vanir gods, is said to rule Alfheim.

Svartalfheim

Svartalfheim or *Svartálfaheimr* is the home of the dwarves who are craftsmen and master smiths who live underground. The realms are thought of a subterranean complex of forges and mines. However, one source (Snorri) described this realm as the home of the black elves.

Hel

Hel is the home of the goddess Hel and generally used to refer to the underworld where the dead dwells. Like the Tartarus in Greek Mythology, Hel is also said to be guarded by a large dog.

Aside from the dwellers of the Nine Worlds, other beings are said to live under, on, or in the giant ash tree. In the poem *Grímnismál,* an Eddic poem that means "The Song of the Hooded

One" the inhabitants in Yggdrasil were briefly mentioned including an eagle that perches in the upper branches of the ash tree and the dragon known as Nidhogg that gnaws at the tree's roots. Meanwhile, the highest shoots are nibbled by four deers: Dyranthror, Duneyr, Dvalin, and Dain. Ratatosk is a squirrel that carries messages between the anonymous eagle and Nidhogg.

The Essence of Yggdrasil

The Well of Urd and Yggdrasil are core aspects of the Nordic mythology that portray the Viking perception of something instead of an actual description of a place. Scholars believe that these two don't refer to one location, but instead they are at the core of everything and anything.

Basically, this portrayal expresses the native Nordic perception on the essence of time and destiny. In a study entitled *The Well and the Tree: The World and Time in Early Germanic Culture* the author Paul Bauschatz suggests that the Well and the Tree correspond to the two tenses of the Germanic languages.

For example, English is a Germanic language that has two major tenses:

1. The present tense that describes events that are happening now (e.g. He is eating).

2. The past tense that includes events that already happened (e.g. He ate) as well as events that started in the past and are still happening (e.g. He has been eating).

Not similar to Romance languages such as French or Spanish, for instance, Germanic languages do not have a future tense. Rather, they are using specific verbs in the present tense to express futurity such as shall or will. (He shall eat or He will eat).

Instead of futurity these verbs express the necessity or the intention.

Yggdrasil corresponds to the present tense that is still happening now. In turn, the Well of Urd corresponds to the past tense as it serves as the storage of finished or ongoing activities that nourishes Yggdrasil and boosts its growth.

The Nordic perception of time is cyclical and not linear. The Vikings believe that past events can affect present events and the other way around. The present can return to the past that retroactively changes the chain. In turn, the new past is reabsorbed into a new present that moves through the flow of the water from the well to the tree.

With this framework, we can better understand the Viking perception of destiny. The Norns, or the residents of the Well of Urd, have designed the earliest form of the destinies of all creatures who are living in the Nine Realms found in Yggdrasil. However, all beings can choose to shape their own destiny as well as the destinies of people around them. This is perceived as the dew that falls back into the Well of Urd.

Beings can accept their fate passively or actively shape them through magic. In the Nordic belief system, magic is perceived as the process of getting a higher degree of control over someone's destiny. Vikings believe that there is no absolute fate as there is no absolute free will. Rather, they believe that life is somewhere between these two extremes.

Creation as a Cycle

Scholars regard the Nordic creation story as one of the most vivid accounts in literature. Aside from its colorful and interesting plot - it is also filled with subtle distinctions. Below is the creation myth as believed by the Vikings:

Before the creation of the sky, land, and sea, there was only deep abyss known as Ginnungagap. The English word gap that means empty space or void originated from this Old Norse term. This darkness and calmness lay between Niflheim (the realm of ice) and Muspelheim (the realm of fire).

The billowing flames from Muspelheim and the frost from Niflheim met in the dark abyss until the ice was melted and the water drops became Ymir or the first giant, who has both genders and can spawn more giants through his sweat.

The second being to be created in the melting spot was Audhumbla or a cow that nourished Ymir. Audhumbla licked the ice until the first Aesir god, Buri, emerged. Bor, the son of Buri, married Bestla, the daughter of Bolthorn the giant. The couple had children named Odin, Vili and Ve. Odin became the chief of the Aesir tribe gods.

The world was created when Odin and his siblings slew Ymir. The sky was made from his skull, his brains became the clouds, his hair became the trees and plants, his muscles and skin became the land, and his blood turned into ocean. The gods then created the first man and woman named Ask and Embla, and they have constructed a fence around their homeland, Midgard, to protect them from the realm of the giants.

One of the subtle meanings of the Nordic cosmology is that creation never happens from nothing. Chaos and destruction is necessary for creation. Death springs life - a concept that is evident each time we eat. The Norse creation story prominently features the constant reciprocity as a core concept of life. The world, from the perception of the Vikings, is not created out of nothing in contrast with the creation story of the Judeo-Christian world. The slaying of the giant Ymir was necessary to create the world. Each time the Vikings ate, destroy lands to establish settlements, or join raids and battles, they are inspired by the concept of chaos as necessary in bringing new life.

Moreover, the Norse creation story is a cycle and not a linear event. In the Judeo-Christian world, the creation was a major event that happened in the past, and was accomplished by one being - the Unmoved Mover, God, Yahweh- who holds all the power for creation as well as destruction.

The Norse creation story features the initial creation of the world as they believe that the process is continuous as manifested by the essence of Yggdrasil and the Well of Urd. All dwellers of the Nine Realms, even the giants, play a role in the creation process.

Afterlife

The mythology of the Nordic people doesn't feature any solid doctrine about the afterlife. According to Hilda Ellis Davidson, an English antiquarian, there's no clear image in Norse mythology about where people go when they die. But still, archaeological and literary sources present discernible patterns that provide us images on how the Nordic people perceive death and the afterlife.

For example, literary sources often mention Valhalla or the Hall of the Fallen in Old Norse as a place where fallen warriors go when they die in battle. Valhalla is the magnificent hall owned by the Aesir god Odin who collects warriors to celebrate with him until they are called to battle at Ragnarok.

The goddess Freya also has a hall for the dead called Folkyang or the Field of the People. Unlike Valhalla, there is not enough mentioned of Folkyang in literary sources. Those who died at sea are taken underwater to join the giantess Ran.

On the other hand, Helgafjell or Holy Mountain was believed to be another place for people who have not died in battle, but lived a good life. Those people who died dishonorably are believed to go to Helheim, which is a dark and cold place ruled by the Goddess Hel. For Vikings, dying in your bed because of laziness or old age is the worst way to die.

CHAPTER THREE

VALHALLA

Valhalla came from the Old Norse word *Valhöll,* which means the *hall of the fallen.* This is generally where Odin, chief of the Aesir gods, houses the souls of the warriors whom he deemed worthy of celebrating with him. Literary sources describe Valhalla as a great hall located in the Asgard – the home of the Aesir gods.

In the Eddic poem Grímnismál or the Song of the Hooded One in reference to Odin, Valhalla is depicted as a splendid place. Its roof is made of shields while the rafters are made of spears. It houses hundreds of feasting tables where the seats of the chosen warriors are made of breastplates. Eagles fly above the hall and wolves guard the gates.

The einherjar or the inhabitants of Valhalla fight each other all day long to impress Odin. Even though they are already dead, they still bleed and get wounded in the process. But every night, the Valkyries heal their wounds and restore them to full health. They prepare for the nightly feast that is really grandeur for Vikings as they enjoy an endless supply of exceptionally fine food and drink. The beautiful Valkyries serve them with meat that came from Saehrimnir, a magical boar that is resurrected each time he is butchered. The chosen warriors also drink a mead from the udder of Heidrun the goat.

But Odin and his warriors know that they are doomed. During Ragnarok, when Odin has to face the wolf Fenrir, he will call the mighty warriors to aid him and fulfill their destiny to be killed in the great battle. Hence, the inhabitants of the great hall are mainly elite warriors, rulers, and heroes of the Viking world.

Gaining Entrance to Valhalla

As mentioned, Odin, through his Valkyries, chose the worthy Viking warriors to enter Valhalla. Those who are not deemed worthy are sent to the Folkvang or the hall of Freya, wife of Odin.

But it is important to remember that scholars such as Daniel McCoy noted that there is no reliable source that exactly describes the selection process to gain entry into Valhalla. Hence, the requirements to gain this reward is not explicit. It can also be said that the Norse afterlife is basically a continuation of life in Midgard and the religion of the Vikings do not judge people based on their morality that is similar to the Christian notion of Heaven and Hell.

It was the Irish scholar Snorri Sturluson that filled the gaps in the Norse religion in the 13th century, which is roughly centuries after Christianity was established in Ireland. Snorri is also a Christian scholar so his imagery could be considered as inspired by the Judeo-Christian concept of afterlife. Snorri wrote that those who died in battle are taken to Valhalla, while those who died of old age or sickness are sent to Hel.

But still, it is fairly logical that Odin would choose the best warriors to fight him during Ragnarok.

The Importance of Valhalla in Norse Mythology

Worshipping the gods is central to the life of the Nordic people. Hence, they regularly perform rituals to appease the divine beings. For example, they made sacrifices to ask for specific blessings such as success in battle, bountiful harvest, or fertility. They also worship the divinity of nature such as water, mountains, and even rocks.

For warriors, Valhalla is the ultimate reward and they are inspired to perform valorous acts during battle to impress Odin. Scholars consider this as the main reason why the Vikings were fierce in every battle. They are merely performing a tryout for a magnificent battle in the afterlife.

Viking warriors are always looking forward to join battles and wars and they don't fear death. For a warrior, it is a great shame to die of old age so even the elderly is keen to join battle to impress Odin and invite them to join Ragnarok.

The Valkyries

The Valkyries are spirit helpers of Odin. They are often depicted as elegant, female maidens that takes the dead warriors to Valhalla. In earlier accounts, the Valkyries are portrayed as sinister beings but in later sources, their imagery was sanitized and usually focused on their romantic affairs with mortal men and their noble duty of helping Odin in taking his chosen warriors to Valhalla and serving them during feasts.

It is also said that Odin permits some Valkyries to transform into pretty white swans, but if a mortal sees the spiritual maiden without the swan disguise, she can no longer go back to Valhalla.

In earlier accounts, Valkyries are not seen as objective players in the battlefield as they are also believed to choose those who will die in battle and even using magic to make certain that the marked ones will die.

In the sagas and the Eddas, there are stories about how Valkyries decide who lives in battle such as a poem included in *Njal's Saga* entitled *Darraðarljóð.* In the poem, there were 12 Valkyries that are seen before the Battle of Clontarf sitting at a loom and then weaving the tragic fate of several warriors. The imagery was quite dark as the spirit maidens used intestines to weave the loom, arrows and swords for beaters, and decapitated heads for weights. Meanwhile, the Volsungsaga compares watching a Valkyrie like "staring into a flame".

This imagery is supported if we explore the lore of other Germanic cultures. For example, Anglo Saxons also have their own version of Valkyries known as the *wælcyrie* who were female spirits of carnage. Meanwhile, the Celts also had similar entities such as the war deities Morrigan and Badb.

CHAPTER FOUR

VIKING DEITIES

T he Viking religion is filled with various beings. Before the dawn of Christianity in the Nordic lands, people believed that humans were not the only inhabitants of the Earth. Everything that is part of nature - plants, animals, rocks, lake, rivers - have their own spirit. The Viking world was also populated with numerous beings who are not visible to the mortal eyes. These invisible beings include the Aesir deities, Vanir deities, giants, elves, dwarves, land spirits, Valkyries, norns, and spirit ancestors.

DEITIES OF THE AESIR TRIBE

The Aesir is one of the two primary tribes worshipped by the Vikings. Many of the popular Norse gods and goddesses are members of the Aesir tribe, including Odin, Frigg, Thor, Loki, Tyr, Heimdall, Idun, Bragi, and Baldur. They dwell in Asgard that is located in the highest branch of Yggdrasil.

Odin is the chief of the Aesir deities, but there are some sources suggesting that this role was first occupied by the god Tyr.

Odin

Odin, also known as Wotan, Woden, or Wodan, is one of the main deities in Norse mythology. However, his exact role and nature can be difficult to discern because of the complex imagery of him given by rich yet opposing literary and archaeological sources.

But in general, Odin is known as the Allfather as he is known as the chief of the gods. He is both an Aesir and a Vanir god. His mother, Bestla, is one of the first frost-giants, so the Allfather also has giant blood in his veins. An Eddic poem also identifies him as the breath of life.

The raven and the wolf are associated to Odin. Sleipnir is his magical horse, which has teeth inscribed with runes, and eight legs that help the being to gallop across wide distances. The Allfather was considered as well-adept in magic and was associated with runes.

Odin is often portrayed as a tall, old man, with a grey flowing beard. He only has one eye as he traded his other eye for wisdom. He is said to wear a wide-brimmed hat, a cloak, and carries a spear.

Even though he rules the Aesir gods that dwell in Asgard, he is noted to venture far from the majestic realm usually on solitary wanderings. He loves wisdom and he continuously seeks it, but there are sources depicting him as a deity that is lacking in respect for law, fairness, or justice. He is indeed an enigmatic deity because while he is respected as the patron of rules, he is also worshipped by outcasts. He is the peaceful god of poetry, yet he is also the fierce god of war.

In modern times, Odin is usually portrayed as a formidable commander in the battlefield and an honorable ruler. But there are archaeological sources suggesting that Odin fades in comparison to noble war gods such as Thor or Tyr. Odin is said to usually incite peaceful folks to chaos. He only bestows his blessings to those who are deemed worthy such as notable heroes, including the Volsung family and Starkaor.

Odin has a close affinity with berserker warriors who are noted for their spiritual fighting techniques and associated with divine practices that revolve around achieving union with specific fierce spirit animals such as bears or wolves, and in some instances, with Odin himself who is also the master of these beasts.

As a war god, Odin is mainly concerned with the frenzy and the chaos that bloodshed brings and not with any noble reason behind any conflict.

Thor

Thor is one of the most popular Norse gods. The Vikings worship Thor because he embodies brawn, loyalty, and honor. He is known as the unshakable defender of Asgard and the Aesir gods against frost giants.

Literary and archaeological sources praise the thunder god's unfaltering sense of duty and courage, and his unmatched physical strength. His magical belt, called *megingjarðar* doubled his strength. However, his most popular possession is Mjöllnir or the Lightning Hammer. Thor is always depicted with this magical hammer.

For the Vikings, Thor is the embodiment of thunder, while Mjöllnir was the embodiment of lightning when the god is fighting the frost giants. Thor's archenemy is Jormungand, the giant sea snake who encroaches Midgard or the realm of human beings.

In one story, Thor tried pulling the sea serpent out of the ocean while he was fishing, but he was stopped by his giant companion. During Ragnarok, Thor and Jormungand will battle against each other in one final battle.

While Thor is the defender against the giants, he himself has giant blood. Odin, his father, is half-giant, while Jord, his mother, is fully descended from the giants. But this kind of ancestry is not uncommon among the Norse gods.

Aside from being a war god, Thor is also worshipped as a god of agriculture and fertility. Scandinavian settlers also prayed to him to hallow the lands before they establish early settlements as suggested by surviving runic inscriptions. He is also admired as the sky god who can control the rain that is crucial for Viking farmers to grow their crops. Sif, the wife of Thor, is depicted as a lady with golden hair as a symbol of rich harvest. The marriage of Thor and Sif is considered as a divine union as it is considered a great blessing during the Viking age that the sky (Thor) and earth (Sif) becomes united and brings fruitful harvest for the land.

Loki

Loki is known as the trickster god in Norse mythology. But technically, Loki is not a god, but a Jotun or a giant. While he is not good, he is also not considered to be evil. Loki lives in Asgard, and originated from Jotunheim or the realms of the giants. He was the son of Laufey and Farbauti who are both giants. He entertains himself by tricking and annoying the Aesir gods and goddesses.

The Vikings call Loki *the sly one* because he is both cunning and clever. He is creative in coming up with new ideas to trick and embarrass the gods as well as mortal beings. For the sake of fun, Loki loves to prank people, but will later save them so he will look like the hero.

One of his major powers is shape shifting into any form he wants. In literary sources, he was noted to transform into an elderly woman, a fly, a seal, a horse, and a salmon.

Loki and Sigyn have two children – Vali and Narvi. But Loki was also married to the giantess Angrboda who gave her three offspring - Jormungand (the archenemy of Thor), Fenrir the Wolf, and Hel the goddess of the underworld. Loki is also considered as a mother as he gave birth to Sleipnir, which is the magical horse of Odin.

Loki is best known for his baleful role in the Death of Baldur. When a prophecy declared that the god Baldur will die, Frigg, his mother, went on a journey to secure the oath from every living thing not to harm her beloved son. However, the goddess ignored the mistletoe, which she thought too small and harmless to cause death. Loki discovered this omission, so Loki fashioned a spear from a mistletoe, and tricked Hod, a blind god, to throw it towards Baldur.

Without the knowledge of the weapon's origin, Hod impaled Baldur. Immediately, Odin instructed the god Hermod to take his horse Sleipnir to go to Hel and ask the goddess Hel to bring back Baldur as he was a beloved being.

Hel, a daughter of Loki, said that she would only release the soul of Baldur if everything would weep for the dead god. All living things wept for Baldur, except for a giantess named Tokk, who was suspected to be Loki in disguise.

As punishment, Odin imprisoned the sly god in a cave with a venomous snake above his head. His faithful wife, Sigyn, accompanied Loki in the cave and held a bowl over the sly god's head to collect the snake's venom. But once the bowl becomes full, the goddess has to leave the cave to pour out the venom. During her absence the drops of poison that falls unto Loki causes him unbearable pain that causes earthquakes.

Frigg

Frigg, also known as Frigga, is the most venerated goddess in Norse Mythology. She is the wife of Odin and as such she is allowed to sit on Allfather's *Hlidskjalf,* or high seat, to look out over the universe. She is the mother to the beloved god Baldur, and the blind god Hod. Frigg is also the stepmother to Vali, Vidar, Bragi, Tyr, Hermod, Hoder, Heimdall, and Thor.

Frigg is described as a *volva* who practices *seidr,* which is a type of Norse magic related to discerning destiny. She is considered as the goddess of motherhood, fertility, marriage, and love.

According to Norse lore, Frigg has three beloved maidens, but he favorite is Fulla whom she entrusts with all her secrets. Fulla is depicted as a lovely maiden wearing a golden snood that she got as a present from Frigga. Another maiden is called Gna or the messenger maiden. Her task is to run errands for Frigga all around the Nine Realms. If she needs to deliver an urgent message, she rides Hofvarpnir another magical horse that can gallop through the ocean. The third maiden is called Hlin whose task is to protect any person or object that is special for Frigga.

Baldur

Baldur, also known as Balder or Baldr, is known as the god of light in Norse mythology. He is well-loved by both the Aesir and Vanir gods, and he is worshipped for his purity. He is the most beautiful god that even the flowers bow down before him. Among the gods, he is the most gracious, fairest, and wisest.

Baldur is the second son of Frigg and Odin. He is the brother of Thor, and the husband of the goddess Nanna, and together they bore the god Forseti. Breidablik is the hall of Baldur, which is known as the brightest house in Asgard. It is said that only beings that are purest can enter Baldur's hall.

The Eddic poems describe the roof of Baldur's hall as made of silver and emanating from gorgeous pillars. Baldur owns a ship known as Hringhorn that was described as the most beautiful ship in Asgard. During his death, the ship was used as his funeral pyre.

Baldur's death is among the most popular stories in Norse mythology. When the god of light began to dream about his demise, his mother Frigg, traveled through all the realms of Ygdrassil to ask every being (living or non-living) to pledge not to harm her beloved son. As a result, Baldur became invincible, so much so that the other gods entertained themselves by throwing weapons and any object at him, but everything just bounced off him as fulfillment for their promise not to harm the god.

The trickster god Loki sensed a chance for mischief. He went to Frigg and asked if she had overlooked anything when she was asking for the divine pledges. It turned out that the goddess thought that the harmless mistletoe was too insignificant that she just skipped it. Loki then fashioned a spear made of mistletoe and persuaded Hodr, the blind god and brother of Baldur, to throw the weapon at Baldur. The spear instantly impaled the god, and he died instantly.

The stricken Asgardians then ordered the god Hermod to quickly travel to the underworld to ask the goddess Hel if there is any chance to resurrect the god of light. When Hermod arrived at Hel, he found Baldur, now grim and pale, sitting in the seat of honor next to the goddess of the underworld. Hermod asked the goddess to let go of Baldur, and after much encouragement, the goddess agreed to revive Baldur if everything in the world would cry for him, to prove the divine claim that the god is universally beloved.

Frigg again quickly travelled around the world to ask everything to weep for the brightest god, and indeed everything wept, except for the giantess named Pokk, who was assumed to be Loki himself. And so, Baldur will forever remain in Hel until the day of Ragnarok comes.

Heimdall

Heimdall is another Aesir god who lives in Asgard. However, he has a particular dwelling known as Himinbjoirg that is said to be located at the highest point in Asgard known as Bifrost. He is the guardian of Asgard, and if there are approaching intruders against Asgard, Heimdall blows the *Gjallarhorn,* or the *yelling horn*. The sound of this great horn is said to be heard throughout the nine realms.

While Heimdall is also the son of Odin, the Eddic poems describe Heimdall as the son of the Nine Waves or the nine maiden sisters, which is noted as the reason why the god has been blessed with multiple gifts. The nine maidens were named *Duva* (the Hidden One), *Kolga* (the Cold One), *Blodughadda* (the Red One), *Bara* (the Foam Fleck), *Bylgja* (Billow Breaker), *Hronn* (Welling Wave), *Hefring* (Rising Wave), *Unn* (Frothing Wave), and *Himinglava* (Transparent Wave).

According to the sagas, the love of the Nine Waves was incomparable, and their loyalty to each other was formidable. So when one of them fell in love and choose to lay with Odin, against the will of Aegir (the god of the sea), the other eight maidens stood by her to defend their sister. Some sources say that Odin bedded all the maidens, which was a courageous act as the sisters were bloodthirsty maidens. One of them later became pregnant with the guardian of the Bifrost.

The Vikings considered Heimdall as the father of all people. Before becoming the guardian of Asgard, he travelled around the world to visit married couples, and stayed with them for three nights. The first couple were servants, the next were farmers, and the last couple were noble. Nine months after the visit, the couples bore children.

The first child was Thrall who was ugly but strong. He became the ancestor of all servants. The second child was Karl who was skilled in agriculture and became the ancestors of farmers. The third child was Jarl who was highly skilled in combat and became the ancestors of warriors.

Tyr

Tyr is the old god of war and considered as the Lawgiver among the Asgardians. The most courageous among the Norse pantheon, it is Tyr who binded Fenrir where he lost his right hand. The gods were worried that the pup Fenrir was quickly growing, so they decided to tie up the wolf pup in fetters.

When Fenrir saw the chain that would bind him, he was suspicious, and declared that he will only be allowed to be binded if one of them would lay an arm in his mouth as a symbol of good faith. As the bravest god, only Tyr agreed to do so. When Fenrir was bounded and failed to break free from the chains, he bit off the arm of the war god.

Before Odin, Tyr was considered as the chief of the Aesir gods. The reason for his demotion is unknown.

Similar to Odin, Tyr has many traits of the early Germanic deities of war. Mentions in other mythologies and archeological evidence related to a one-hand deity, suggest that the character is quite old and has been worshipped in Northern Europe several thousands of years before Snorri Sturluson mentioned the god in the Prose Edda.

Idun

Idun is an Aesir goddess, but there is limited information about her. The only source that prominently mentions her is the story about her kidnapping. In the skaddic tale, Idun is noted as the owner and dispenser of an apple tree that bestows immortality. As such she plays an important role in sustaining the immortality of the Asgardians. The husband of Idun is Bragi, the minstrel and court poet of Asgard.

Bragi

Bragi is the god of poetry and songs who entertain the inhabitants of Asgard, especially Odin and his warriors in Valhalla. However, there are some sources that lay doubt on the status of Bragi as a god, as he is considered a special being among the immortals because of his talent in reciting poetry.

Like the other Norse deities, Bragi is immortal because his wife, the goddess Idun, is the owner and dispenser of the apples that bestows immortality to Asgardians. However, there is no record that Bragi has been worshipped by pre-Christian Norse people similar to the worship of major gods.

Vili and Ve

Vili and Ve are the two brothers of Odin who played a critical role in the shaping of the Nine Realms. The Eddic Poems tell us that the three brothers were the original Aesir gods to exist who slew the giant Ymir and caused the creation of Midgard. However, other scholars believe that Vili, Ve, and Odin are actually one god only in three forms as these names were used interchangeably in many literary resources.

Forseti

The Vikings regard Forseti as the divine law speaker or the god of justice. He is the son of the goddess Nanna and the god Baldur. He dwells in the shining hall of Glitnir with its rood inlaid with decorative silver and the pillars are made of red gold. This hall serves as his court of justice where he settles legal disputes in Asgard. While Forseti is among the major gods of Norse mythology, he is not significantly featured in any of the surviving literary sources.

Gevjun

Gevjun is considered as the goddess of prosperity, abundance, fertility, and agriculture. Her name can be translated as the Generous One or the Giver. In the account of Snorri Sturluson, the goddess visited the modern-day country of Sweden as a homeless woman. He encountered King Gylfi who was noted for his generosity. The King promised to grant her as much land as four oxen can plow in a day, so the deity called her four sons and turned them into oxen to plow the land. Not only that the divine sons plowed the land, they also dragged the land from Sweden that caused a depression and became the Malaren lake. The land was dragged out into the ocean and became the island of Zealand, which is the location today of Copenhagen.

Sif

Sif is the wife of the thunder god Thor. While his husband is more popular than her, Sif was quite a revered goddess in pre-Christian Europe as she was worshipped as a goddess of family, fertility, and wheat. The two primary literary sources that describe Sif are the Prose Edda and the Poetic Edda. She is depicted as a beautiful lady with golden hair. Thor was her second husband as she was first married to Orvandil, which was a giant. She is usually compared to other fertility goddesses such as Frigg and Freya. In the Eddas, Thor was said to be heavily in love with the goddess, especially her beautiful hair that is bright like the sun. It was flawless and flowed down to her back.

In one story, Loki randomly decided to cut off Sif's hair. Thor was enraged and threatened to kill the trickster god, but the sly one convinced the war god to spare his life on the condition that he will replace the golden hair. Thor agreed and Loki searched the world to find new hair for the goddess.

Sif's hair is said to represent wheat, and she blesses the crops of the Nordic farmers. Farmers would worship Sif to protect their crops from winters, cold winds, and pestilence.

Ullr

Ullr is the son of Sif, the goddess of fertility and wheat, and the stepson of Thor, the thunder god. While the giant Orvandil was the first husband of Sif, there is no existing literary or archaeological evidence that mention the giant as Ullr's father.

Norse scholars establish that this Norse god is another war god that is well-skilled in hunting, archery, and skiing. The Poetic Edda also mentions that his home is known as Ydalir of Yew Dales. In making bows, Yew is the preferred wood, which possibly explains this association.

While his mother is depicted as the goddess of wheat and harvest, Ullr is considered as the god of snow.

Hermod

Hermond is another war god in Norse mythology, although not as prominent as Odin, Thor, or Tyr. He is the son of Odin and Frigg, and while he is considered a minor god, he is still a popular one because of the role he played in the story of Baldur's death. When the god of light was killed due to the mischief of Loki, he was the only god in Asgard brave enough to journey to the underworld and encourage Hel to let Baldur go.

Sigyn

Sigyn is an Aesir goddess and the wife of Loki the trickster god. Their sons are Vali and Narfi. When Loki played too much mischief towards the inhabitants of Asgard, Odin punished him to be imprisoned and bound in a cave with a venomous snake over his head. Because of her love to Loki, Sigyn sacrificed her freedom and choose to stay with her husband to hold a bowl above the trickster god's head to collect the venom. But when the bowl is full, Sigyn has to go out of the cave to throw the poison, so some of the drops of venom continued to fall on to Loki's head that causes tremendous pain. His pain causes earthquakes in Midgard or the realm of the humans. Loki will stay imprisoned until Ragnarok and take revenge against Odin.

DEITIES OF THE VANIR TRIBE

Aside from the Aesir, the Vikings also worshipped different deities from the Vanir tribes such as Freya, Freyr, Njord, and Nerthus. The Vanir gods are older than the Aesir gods and they live in Vanaheim, one of the Nine Realms that are held within the branches of Yggdrasil. The Vanir are skilled in magic and sorcery and they are particularly talented in predicting the future. When the war between the Vanir and Aesir ended, three Vanid deities were sent to Asgard - Njord and his children Freyr and Freya.

Freya

Freya is considered as the goddess of love, sex, and beauty in Norse mythology. But she is also associated with fertility, sorcery, wealth, war, and death. The Vanir goddess is also associated with lust. In of the Eddas, Loki accused Freya of having an affair with all the gods as well as elves, including her brother.

The name Freya means lady in Old Norse, and also written as Freiya, Freja, Froya, or Frua. While she is a Vanir goddess, she lives among the Aesir deities after she was sent by the Vanir deities as a token of truce. The Aesir also sent two deities, Mimir and Honir, to the Vanir. As such, Freya became an honorable deity in Asgard after the war between the Vanir and the Aesir ended.

Freya is the daughter of the Vanir god Njord and Nerthus. His twin brother is Freyr. Freya's husband is the Vanid god Odr, but he was said to disappear so Freya became another wife of Odin. With Odr, Freya had two children names Gersimi and Hnoss.

As a divine practitioner of the Norse magic seidr, Freya is considered as a volva like the Aesir goddess Frigg. In fact, she brought to Asgard and Midgard the practice of this organized form of magic that can control and manipulate prosperity, health, and desires. In Asgard, she resides in her hall known as the Folkvang, where like Odin, she also chooses her warriors to aid her battle once Ragnarok comes.

Freyr

Freyr is the twin brother of Freya, who was depicted in the Eddas as a gorgeous deity and associated with good harvest, wealth, and prosperity. When the war between the Aesir and Vanir ended, Freyr with his sister Freya and his father Njord were sent to Asgard as a token of peace. Freyr is also the Lord of the Elves and he reigns in Alfheim, the realm of the Elves. His wife is the giantess Gerd from Jotunheim.

According to legend, Freyr is said to be seriously in love with the giantess. It all started when one day, Freyr sneaked up to sit in Odin's throne where anyone can see a view of the Nine Realms. When the Vanir god looked at the direction of Jotunheim, he saw a beautiful giantess and he immediately fell in love.

Freyr learned that Gerd's father is the giant called Gymir who was hostile to the Vanir and the Aesir. Thinking he had no chance to pursue Gerd, the god felt so bad that he would not even eat or speak, so his health deteriorated. Njord, his father, got so worried about his son's behavior.

Njord sent Skirnir, his servant to check why his son was so sad. Upon returning to the elder god, the servant told him about the feelings of Freyr to the giantess. Njord immediately commanded Skirnir to travel to Jotunheim and propose a marriage to Gerd.

Skirnir borrowed Freyr's magical sword to protect himself while in Jotunheim. When the servant arrived at the house of Gymir and announced the intention of Freyr to marry his daughter, the giant replied that his daughter is old enough to decide. To convince Gerd, Skirnir presented apples from Idun that can bestow immortality to anyone who eats them. But Gerd rejected the proposal and the apples.

Next, Skirnir offered the golden ring called Draupnir, which is magical because every nine days, it would produce eight more rings that are of equal quality. Again, Gerd was not impressed and still rejected the offer. Skirnir changed his strategy and instead threatened the giantess that if the proposal will be rejected for a third time, the Vanir would curse her and her father using secret runes.

Gymir and Gerd were frightened by the threat and accepted the proposal, but in one condition. Freyr has to wait for nine days before the wedding. This nine day wait was the giantess' way to torture the feelings of Freyr. After nine days, the two still got married.

Njord

Njord is a Vanir god that is associated with wealth, inland waters, coasts, seafarers, and wind. Together with his children, Freyr and Freya, the Vanir sent him to the Aesir tribe of gods as a token of truce. He lives in a house near a coast in Asgard named Noatun or Ship Haven.

While Njord is married to the giantess Skadi, he slept with his sister named Nerthus and together they had two children - Freyr and Freyr. Njord is often mistaken as the god of the sea, which is not accurate because the Nordic people worshipped Aegir as the sea god.

While the Vanir permitted the union of Njord and Nerthus, the Aesir did not tolerate marriage between brothers and sisters. Hence, Njord had to marry Skadi. As the story goes, Skadi attacked Asgard. To avoid conflict, the Aesir gods proposed that she could marry any god of his choice in one condition - she should choose by only seeing their feet. Skadi was eyeing for Baldur, which is the most handsome among the god. However, Njord has the most beautiful feet, so he was chosen by Skadi.

As the legend goes, the couple could not agree on where they would live. Skadi hated the seashore, while Njord hated the cold realm of Jotunheim. After spending nine nights at each place, they decided to go back to their own homes.

Nerthus

Nerthus is a popular Germanic deity that is associated with fertility. This goddess is depicted by Tacitus, a Roman historian from the 1st century AD in his work Germania. In the ethnographic work of Tacitus, he mentioned the union of the Suebi tribes as they venerated the goddess Nerthus by maintaining a sacred grove and a holy wagon draped with cloth that only priests could touch. The presence of the goddess is said to dwell in the old wagon that is drawn by the heifers. The sacred wagon is paraded in towns where people would welcome the group with peace and celebration. All arms are locked away, so there will be no war. However, the culmination of this peaceful celebration is horrifying as the cart and the cloth are washed by the slaves in a secluded lake. The slaves are sacrificed by the priests by drowning them.

These depictions - the wagon that are paraded from town to town and the locking of weapons during the celebration are strongly associated with the Vanir deities who reigned over peace and prosperity. Human sacrifice is also practiced in the Norse religion.

GIANTS

While the ancient Nordic peoples mainly worshipped the Aesir and the Vanir gods and goddesses, they also believed in the existence of the giants who are equally powerful with the gods. However, the character of the giants is quite different from the deities and in fact, they are seen as opposing yet intertwined forces that balance the cosmology.

While these beings are called giants, they are not necessarily enormous in size like what we usually think about when we hear the term. In fact, the name giant in reference to the beings who dwell in Jotunheim is a misleading name. In modern English, a giant is a being that is enormous in size. But during the Viking times, the word giant is used to refer to a being that is powerful but dreaded as opposed to the gods that are powerful but adored.

In Old Norse, the giants are called jotnar or jotun. When England was conquered by William the Conqueror in 1066 AD, the English language was filled with Norman (French) terms. One of the terms that was used during those times was the Old French geant, which is the origin of the modern English term giant. This replaced the Old English word jotun.

Geant was used to refer to the giants in the Greek myth who were also the enemies of the gods similar to the jotun in Norse. The Greek origin of geant also was used to translate a Hebrew term that refers to beings that are huge in physical size. And so, this became the dominant meaning of the word.

Below are the prominent giants in the Norse mythology.

Fenrir

Fenrir is not a pure blood giant. He is the son of the god Loki and Angrboda who was a giantess. Hence, he is the brother of the goddess Hel and the serpent Jormungand - the archenemy of Thor. While he is not a pure blood giant, he is considered as the most prominent giant because he is seen as the doom of the gods who will wreak havoc in the Nine Realms when Ragnarok comes.

As told in the story of The Binding of Fenrir, the Aesir deities are aware of Fenrir's power, so they have decided to raise him as a young pup to control him. But his growth was astonishingly quick and eventually the worried deities decided to bind him up. With his unbelievable strength, Fenrir easily broke through the chains during their first two attempts. The deities asked the dwarves to forge the strongest fetters to help hold him down.

As master craftsman, the dwarves fashioned a chain that is light and soft but can really hold the Fenrir. The gods told Fenrir that they are only playing a game. But when they presented the third chain, the young pup became suspicious and refused to be bound unless one of the gods would stick an arm inside his mouth. Tyr the brave god volunteered, and when Fenrir wasn't able to break free from the fetters, he ripped off the god's arm. That is why the god Tyr is depicted as the one-arm god.

The magical chain was then tied to a boulder, and the deities placed a sword in the wolf's jaws to hold them open. According to prophecy, he will be free when Ragnarok comes and will kill Odin to take his revenge then will wreak havoc across the Nine Realms.

Skadi

Skadi, also known as Skathi, Skadhi, or Skade, is a frost giantess and often associated with winter. Her husband is the Vanir god Njord. When the Aesir gods killed her father, Thiazi, she attacked Asgard to take revenge. To avoid further conflict, the gods proposed a marriage with one of the gods. Skadi was free to choose any god she likes, but can only choose based on the appearance of their feet. She selected the most beautiful pair of feet thinking they were the feet of the handsome god Baldur. However, it turned out that the feet belonged to Njord a less handsome and older Vanir god of the wind.

Skadi is often portrayed as a winter huntress wearing skis or snowshoes. She is also a sorceress, but she is not an evil goddess.

Ymir

Ymir is a giant that played an important role in the Norse cosmology. Based on the account of the medieval scholar Snorri Sturluson, the giant Ymir was born when the ice from Niflheim and the fire from Muspelheim met in the abyss of Ginnungagap.

The second being to be created in the melting spot was Audhumbla or a cow that nourished Ymir. Audhumbla licked the ice until the first Aesir god, Buri, emerged. Bor, the son of Buri, married Bestla, the daughter of Bolthorn the giant. The couple had children named Odin, Vili and Ve. Odin became the chief of the Aesir tribe gods.

The world was created when Odin and his siblings slew Ymir. The sky was made from his skull, his brains became the clouds, his hair became the trees and plants, his muscles and skin became the land, and his blood turned into ocean. The gods then created the first man and woman named Ask and Embla, and they have constructed a fence around their homeland, Midgard, to protect them from the realm of the giants.

Hel

Although technically a goddess, Hel is identified as a giantess who rules over the underworld that is also called Hel. Her father is the trickster god Loki and the giantess Angrboda. Thus, she is the sister of the world serpent Jormungand and the wolf Fenrir.

The goddess of the underworld is often depicted as indifferent, cruel, harsh, and greedy. However, there is no elaborate description of the goddess in the surviving Norse literature, and she is only mentioned passively in major stories. She is described as being half-white and half-black, with a fierce yet grim facial expression.

Hel played a prominent role in the legend of the Death of Baldur. After the death of the god of light, the stricken Asgardians ordered the god Hermod to quickly travel to the underworld to ask the goddess Hel if there is any chance to resurrect the god of light. When Hermod arrived at Hel, he found Baldur, now grim and pale, sitting in the seat of honor next to the goddess of the underworld. Hermod asked the goddess to let go of Baldur, and after much encouragement, the goddess agreed to revive Baldur if everything in the world would cry for Baldur, to prove the divine claim that the god is universally beloved.

Baldur's mother, the goddess Frigg, quickly travelled around the world to ask everything to weep for the brightest god, and indeed everything wept, except for the giantess named Pokk, who was assumed to be Loki himself. And so, Baldur remained in Hel until the day of Ragnarok comes.

Jormungand

Jormungand is known as the Midgard Serpent or a Dragon who encircles the realm of the mortal humans. He is an enormous being and he is one of the three children of the giantess Angrboda and the trickster god Loki. His siblings are Hel and Fenrir.

His archenemy is Thor the god of thunder. The Eddas are filled with stories about the battles between Jormungand and Thor. In one story, Thor caught the giant serpent but fails to pull him up when Hymir (a giant) worried that it will cause Ragnarok cuts the line and sends back the serpent to the ocean. It is destined that when Ragnarok comes, the two enemies will kill each other.

Nidhogg

Nidhogg is a flying serpent or a dragon who lives under Yggdrasil and devouring its roots. This is damaging the world tree that holds the Nine Realms of the Cosmos. The intention of Nidhogg is to pull the world back to chaos, and he, along with other reptilian giants such as Jormungand, are classified as giants or devourers.

This devourer also plays a prominent role in Ragnarok, in which the giants will overcome the Aesir and Vanir gods. In Voluspa, an Old Norse poem, Nidhogg is said to fly out from under the Yggdrasil when Ragnarok comes to help the giants slay the gods.

In the same poem, Nidhogg is described as the ruler of a region in the underworld known as Nastrond or the

Land of the Corpses where adulterers, murderers, and perjurers are punished.

ELVES

Aside from the gods and giants, the Vikings also believed in the existence and even worshipped the elves, who are portrayed as demigods and luminous beings that are generally friendly to humans. Like the gods and goddesses, the elves are adored by Nordic people.

However, there is no clear distinction that defines the difference between the elves and other spiritual beings such as the gods and the giants. But scholars believe that the elves are more closely associated with the Vanir deities, mainly because Freyr, a god from the Vanir tribe was considered as the Lord of the Elves as he is the ruler of the Alfheim or the realm of the Elves.

While the elves are seen as friendly to humans, they can also cause illnesses if they are disrespected. They also have the power of healing especially if the human humbly repents for their wrong doings and if they have offered sacrifices. Some sources say that elves and humans can interbreed and produce children with human appearance but are gifted with extraordinary powers. Some humans can even become elves after they die.

While medieval laws prohibited the practice of worshipping deities and elves, the literature of the time are filled with stories and legends depicting contact between elves and humans.

DWARVES

The Vikings also believed in the existence of the dwarves who are also referred to as dark elves. They are depicted as small and ugly creatures as they thought to originate from the maggots from the corpse of the giant Ymir. The dwarves dwell under mountains, and their realm is known as the Nidavellir or Svartalfheim.

While they are seen as lesser beings compared to elves, they are adored for their richness as they hold the secret treasures buried underground. They are also highly skilled as blacksmiths as they have the natural talent to craft jewelry and weapons that are incomparable. Many of the weapons and jewelries used by the Aesir and Vanir gods were said to be fashioned by the dwarves. For example, the magical chain that was used to bind Fenrir was made by the dwarves.

Some dwarves also practice magic that they use to enhance the powers of their weapons. They love treasures and precious gems so they often spend a lot of time digging and mining.

CHAPTER FIVE

ARCHAEOLOGICAL SOURCES

O ur present knowledge of the Norse religion and other Germanic folks including the Vikings has been diligently brought together from a wide variety of sources discovered by scholars and historians.

Without a doubt, the most important category among these archaeological sources are the literature that depicts historical and mythological characters that are written in Old Norse between 800 to 1400 BCE, which is a period that involves the era that we now call the Medieval Times and the Viking Age.

The people of Iceland and Scandinavia preserved their religion far longer compared to other Germanic tribes. Icelanders in fact are known for their folk lore's even after the island converted to Christianity. Thanks to the sagas, treaties, and poems that they have preserved, we now enjoy the rich world of the Nordic people that could have been lost.

The stories, legends, and characters of the Norse mythology are mainly from the Icelandic Sagas, the Prose Eddas, and the Poetic Eddas.

ICELANDIC SAGAS

Although the reference of history as an accurate account of events might be different from our present standards, the Icelanders during the Middle Ages have written a diverse source that significantly enriches our present knowledge of the religion and traditions of the Nordic people. Examples of the Icelandic sagas are Landnamabok (Book of Settlements) that is written by an anonymous writer, and the Islendingabok (Book of Icelanders) written by the priest Ari Thorgilsson.

The Icelandic sagas were mainly recorded in the 13th and 14th centuries and tells the stories of popular Germanic folk heroes, Scandinavian kings, and Icelanders. The genre is considered as bare as the Icelandic landscape, and the events are portrayed in a stark way that leaves to the intuition and imagination of the reader.

Even though the elements of the Nordic religion are mentioned, they are done so in a casual manner and often in a passive way as opposed to the more direct style in the poetic Eddas. However, the Saga of the Ynglings, is considered as a notable exception because the first several chapters provide a comprehensive exposition of the deeds and the characters of most Norse gods and goddesses.

THE POETIC EDDAS

Poets who spoke Old Norse have left us numerous significant clues about their religious view. However, the collection of poems called today as the Elder Eddas or the Poetic Eddas, contain thorough exposition of Norse mythology. Examples of these poems, Grimnismal (The Song of the Hooded One) and Voluspa (The Insight of the Seeress), provide rich accounts of the Norse mythology and cosmology.

THE PROSE EDDAS

The Prose Eddas are mainly treaties that were written in the 13th century by the scholar Snorri Sturluson, long after the island converted into Christianity. Hence, the accounts could be enriched through a Christian perspective and the original memories could have been faded.

Snorri referenced the poems contained in the Poetic Edda, but he added a significant amount of information that are not included in the poems. In some verses, he cross-references from other poems that have been lost in history, and in some instances, he just added his own assertions.

Many of these could be verified by reading other sources, and most of Snorri's uncorroborated claims are aligned with the general world view of Norse mythology that makes the scholastic community more inclined to embrace the 13th century accounts. But we can't dismiss the fact that many of Snorri's assertions appear to be basic rationalizations, and it appears that he was trying to reconcile the old mythology with Christian views.

While it would be rash to simply dismiss everything in the Prose Edda that the earlier poems haven't already told us, it would be equally presumptuous to accept every statement of Snorri's at face value. Unfortunately, the latter approach was common throughout much of the nineteenth and twentieth centuries, and as a result most popular introductions to Norse mythology uncritically rehash Snorri's contentions and thereby present a skewed portrait of the old gods and tales.

OTHER ARCHAEOLOGICAL SOURCES

Scholars also used other sources to corroborate or enrich the accounts provided in Old Norse literature. One popular source is the Gesta Danorum written by the Danish scholar Saxo Grammaticus in 12th century. This source includes varieties of many of the legends contained in the Old Norse sources and even several stories that are not verified.

Also in the 1st century BCE, Tacitus, a popular Roman historian, wrote an account concerning the traditions and practices of the Germanic tribes. This is known as De Origine Et Situ Germanorum or the Origin and Situation of the Germanic Peoples, or shortly known as Germania. This book contains rich descriptions of the religious practices of the Germanic tribes who lived in the northern part of the Roman empire.

Meanwhile, the literature of the Anglo-Saxons also contained reliable mythological parallels to some of the stories that are cited in Old Norse sources. This includes Beowulf - the epic poem written in Old English and the Latin account Historia Ecclesiastica Gentis Anglorum or "The Ecclesiastical History of the English People" written by Venerable Bede in the 8th century. These sources also contained several clues about the pre-Christian religions practices of the Anglo Saxons, which is a branch of the Germanic tribe.

Continental Germans also left us the epic poem Nibelungenlied that contains the pre-Christian traditions such as those found in the Merseburg Charms that are spells or prayers that are written in Old High German.

OUR KNOWLEDGE OF NORSE MYTHOLOGY IS NOT COMPLETE

Our present knowledge of the religion and traditional practices of the Nordic people is not complete as many of the sources were written between 12th and 13th century, which is long after the Nordic lands were converted into Christianity. Also, the authors such as Snorri Sturluson and Tacitus are not first-hand writers, and they might have added their own assertions.

Of course, we currently know numerous things about the Norse religion, but there are still haps in the current information that could even change our view of this rich perspective.

CHAPTER SIX

VIKING MAGICAL PRACTICES & BELIEFS

For the pre-Christian Norse and other Germanic tribes, magic was part of their daily living. They believe that magic is a way to work with the fundamental principles of the cosmos and not a way to alter the reality. Magic, in the Norse perspective, is far away to our conception of magic that dwells on illusions or the use of cards or hats for tricks. Their practice of Magic focuses on the level of knowledge that a person understands about the Norse cosmology. Magic during the Viking Age is a form of gathering knowledge.

That is why the magical vocabulary of the Old Norse heavily revolves around knowledge. For example, the Old Norse verb *kunna* both means to have insight or to understand by heart. Another term is *fjolkyngi* that is also derived from *kunna*, which means great knowledge.

Knowing one's destiny is another form of knowledge or magic that the Norse people used to practice. In the Norse perspective, destiny cannot be changed, in comparison to the Greek view of fate. Instead, those people who know their destiny can pursue any means to change its course. For example, even though the Aesir and Vanir gods already know that they are destined to die when Ragnarok comes, they still prepare for the final battle and don't succumb to melancholy.

MAGIC OF THE RUNES

The term rune is an Old Norse word that means holding a secret. This is a form of dangerous magic in the hands of someone who has not mastered its secrets as described in the sagas. The verses warned against the dangers of using the magic of runes without enough knowledge. It requires a great deal of study and practice before one can harness the power of the runes. Even Odin the Allfather had to sacrifice his one eye to obtain wisdom from the runes. He also had to undergo physical pain by spending nine days without food and hung pierced by a spear in the world tree.

The Vikings believe that runes had magical powers. They can be used in casting magic spells to alter the weather, enhance the qualities of its owner, or take a glimpse of destiny. However, many of the runic inscriptions are used to aid people in hunting, farming, or war. Norse people also practiced rune casting, in which the rune counters made of bones or wood are used to get answer from an oracle. The rune counters are thrown and a seer can interpret the future based on how the counters landed.

Pre-Christian Norse folk also used runes for their health. For example, in the Egil's saga, the hero used runes to heal a young girl who has been cursed by a sorceress. Egil made new runic inscriptions, placed them under the girl's pillow and so the girl was healed. Hence, the runes are used as tools to do the bidding of the caster and not necessarily good or evil.

NORSE SHAMANISM

Shamanism is a common practice in the pre-Christian civilizations across Asia, Europe, Americas, and Africa. In general, shamanism is the practice that involves a shaman (practitioner of shamanism) to reach altered states of consciousness to perceive and connect with the spiritual world and deliver message or see the future.

In Norse shamanism, the fundamental principles are similar, although shamans are usually women in ancient Scandinavia. This is also practiced by men but in rare occasions. Male Norse shamans are usually dedicated to a particular deity and normally to aid in war. Hence, in Norse religion, shamanism is mainly practiced by women for the welfare of the whole tribe for hunting, farming, connecting with the spiritual world, divination, and healing.

However, the chief of the Aesir gods, Odin, is depicted as an archetype of a shaman. The story of how he sacrificed his one eye and survived while hanging on Yggdrasil, without food or water, and wounded by his own spear, for nine days to achieve secret wisdom is a shamanistic ritual. The practices of Odin and how he travels around the spiritual realms are well documented in many legends and sagas such as the Ynglinga Saga. Odin is said to travel to the underworld to look for answers, which is quite typical in shamanism, journeying to the other realms to connect with deities or the spirits of the dead.

Like a shaman, Odin also has animal familiars, which are beings that help him in the journeys to the other realms, guiding shaman with knowledge, providing him advice, or connect with other shamans. Odin has his two ravens called Huginn and Muninn and the wolves Freki and Geri.

Norse shamans had to undergo a ritual of death and resurrection to obtain their powers. This can be physical death or while in trance, losing one's life and coming back with a new body that is younger and healthier to continue the work of the shaman.

SEIDR

Seidr is another form of Norse magic that is concerned with the discernment and alteration of the course of destiny by re-weaving the whole or part of the web. Both men and women can practice this type of magic, although females are more widely attested. In most instances, these magical practitioners have their own followers who assist them in certain rituals.

In Norse mythology, it is said that even Odin is an adept in this form of magic after learning it from the goddess Freya who is a member of the Vanir tribe that is more associated with shamanism and other forms of ancient magic.

But in the Viking Age, the practice of seidr is connected with being unmanly or effeminate because its manipulative aspects could oppose the ideal of being direct and open. Viking men are more comfortable in practicing the magic of the runes, so seidr is usually practiced by women that were called volva.

The volvas usually travel from one town to another or from one settlement to another to practice magic and perform prophecies in exchange of food, board, or other trade terms. They travel through the guidance of their animal familiars and they went to where they are needed. Hence, shamans are considered wanderers with no permanent dwellings as corroborated by the archeological findings in Pavlov and Dolni sites in modern-day Czech Republic.

Norse Totemism

Totemism is a form of religious belief practiced by shamanic tribes such as the Norse, in which the humans are said to have a mythical connection with a spiritual being such as a plant or an animal.

For the Norse and other pre-Christian tribes in Europe, totemism has been practiced in two certain powerful areas, which are the animal spiritual guides known as Fylgjur and the patron animals of warriors who are invoked to aid them during battles.

In European legends, the witches are often accompanied by cats or ravens. This is something that originates from an ancient past, as shamans are usually guided by familiar spirits not only cats or ravens but by other animals you can think of. These spirit guides helped each person, and while in trance, these creatures helped the shamans to better understand their ways and follow them to whatever quest they want to take. These animals were known as Fylgjur.

Even the Norse gods and goddesses have their own animal familiars. Odin is specifically associated with horses, ravens, and wolves, while Freyr and Freya have their natural affinity with wild boars, and Thor has been associated with goats. Hence, it is not surprising that the Vikings also had their personal totems.

PHILOSOPHICAL VIEW OF THE NORSE RELIGION

While the Norse pantheon are filled with gods and goddesses that are powerful and mighty, there is no single being that is considered supreme. Even Odin, known as the All Father, is not whole. In order to obtain wisdom from the runes, he had to sacrifice his one eye. While immortal, he is still destined to die when Ragnarok comes.

The Norse deities were subject to limitations. Because the Vikings worshipped numerous gods and goddesses, each with role and personality that is different from the others, no one being possessed all the powers that were attributed to the gods. Some gods are responsible for blessing the livestock, crops, farms, some goddesses bless people with fertility or prosperity, some gods are wiser, and some gods are better warriors.

The Vikings believe that their gods are much like humans, just powerful and immortal. Even the psyche of the gods did not separate them from the physical world, or for that matter, from humans. Even though the Norse believe that their gods are spiritual, they still manifest themselves in physical phenomena. In religious philosophy, this is known as the manifestation of the sacred or hierophant or the manifestation of a god or theophany.

For example, the Vikings felt the presence of Thor when the sky is dark and stormy and thunder and lightning echoes through the wind. On the other hand, Thor's wife, Sif, is depicted as a goddess with long, golden hair that symbolizes ripe wheat. Hence, Sif is the goddess of grain, and the storms that fertilizes the land is basically a symbolism of their marriage.

We can't consider this as pantheism, which is the concept that the physical world or all of nature is divine. There's no indication that the Norse see the physical world as a whole manifested by the deities. However, there are clues pointing out to their belief that parts of the physical world are thought to embody the Norse pantheon.

Because the Norse deities were believed to have human traits and appearance, and because they thought to regularly manifest themselves and even intervene in the affairs of the world, it was possible for the deities and humans to interact with each other. These interactions were a crucial part of the Norse religion. This happened in many various ways, the most intimate of which was the belief that the deities had sexual relationship with humans to establish heroic and royal families.

As a cornerstone of Norse religion, ritual sacrifice is considered as the most common interaction between the deities and humans. The Vikings are pragmatic people, and they did not only believe and worship their gods because of fear or love. They do so because they wanted something in return.

Similar to human connections, if you would like to obtain something from someone - at least in a manner that sustains a healthy relationship between the two - you need to be reciprocal. Because the deities are believed to have human characteristics, if the Vikings are asking for a favor from the gods, they had to give them something that is valuable. This is the reason behind the ritual practices and sacrifices. By offering gifts, the Vikings expected to receive favors in return such as safe winds, rich harvest, more children, or healing from pestilence.

The reciprocal relationship between the Vikings and their deities reflects the sterner human relationships between a warrior and his chieftain. Viking warriors are expected to fight bravely and offer his loyalty and fealty for the chieftain. In return, he will be rewarded with his fair share of the spoils from raids or battles. In spite of the unequal status between the chieftain and the warrior, as well as the unequal status between the deities and the humans, both parties are expected to fulfill their obligations. The chieftain had obligations to the warrior, who in turn had obligations to his chief; and the gods had obligations to humans, but the humans in return had obligations to the divine. Once humans performed the proper rituals and sacrifices, they could expect the gods to bless them with favors.

CHAPTER SEVEN

VIKING INFLUENCE ON POPULAR CULTURE TODAY

Through popular books and films, we thought that the Vikings were barbaric, seafaring raiders who attacked settlements across Europe. However, through recent discoveries, scholars suggest that they are part of a civilized world with their own political structure language, religion, practices, and rich history.

The Viking Age is a crucial part of world history, and these ancient tribes have contributed a lot to our modern way of living from seafaring, language, literature, and many more.

Shipbuilding and Seafaring

The Viking advanced shipbuilding practices is perhaps the most prominent legacy of the Nordic people. With their signature longboats, the Vikings were able to travel around Europe and conquer settlements. The longboats are small wooden vessels with rows of oars along the side and shallow hulls. These were lighter, faster, and easier to maneuver compared to ships from England.

Aside from shipbuilding technology, the Vikings were also great navigators by using advanced tools such as the sun compass that uses calcite crystals to find the position of the sun even during misty days or even after sunset. These innovations later influenced modern seafaring.

Language

In the process of attacks and raids against England, Vikings influenced the British land, culture, and language. Aside from raids, the Vikings also interacted with early British settlers through trading, farming, and also through intermarriage. Many Norse tribes, especially from Scandinavia, migrated to the British Isles, which had a significant influence on the formation of the modern English language.

Hence, the Old Norse also influenced Old English. For example, the suffix - by refers to the Scandinavian village or homestead. Hence, the places Derby, Thorny, and Grimsby were of Viking origins. Another popular example is the Old Norse word berserker, which means bearskin or bear shirt. The berserkers are Viking warriors who invoke Odin during battle by whipping themselves into a frenzied trance during battles.

The following are the English words that originated from Old Norse: arm, bag, cake, child, die, egg, fellow, guest, husband, knife, law, mistake, outlaw, plow, race, rot, sky, troll, ugly, want, weak, and window.

Perhaps, the most popular influence of the Viking language and culture to the English language is the origin of names of four days of the week. Tuesday is named after Tiu or Tyr, Wednesday is Woden or Odin's day, Thursday is Thor's day, and Friday is Freya's day. Some sources suggest that Friday is named after Frigg or Frigg's day.

Literature

The Norse sagas and mythology has heavily influenced many literary figures who wrote their masterpieces in the the English language. For example, J.R.R. Tolkien, the great author of classic tales of The Lord of the Rings, the Hobbit and the Silmarillion, was revealed to be a fan of Norse mythology. His characters especially the depiction of humans, elves, dwarves, and dragons within his tales are significantly influenced by the stories and legends of the Nordic people.

Meanwhile, Fenrir Greyback, a minor villain from the Harry Potter series was derived from Fenrir the Wolf. Students of Hogwarts also take ancient runes as one of their subjects.

In addition, the creators of Marvel franchise also used the character of Thor in their comics as one of the major superheroes and member of the Avengers. These popular literary pieces helped in the propagation of the Norse myth to be alive even thousands of years after Scandinavia converted to Christianity and the church has outlawed the worship and adoration of the Nordic pantheon and practices.

Trade and Economy

Aside from raids, the Vikings also established crucial trade routes not only around Europe but also to far off countries such as China, India, Middle East, and Russia. They started trade routes down to the Dnepropetrovsk and pioneered routes to the Byzantine Empire while also maintaining trades with the Baltic and the Francs.

The modern trading landscape could be very different today, without the work of the Vikings in global trade. Some cities such as Dublin could be non-existent if the Vikings did not reach its shores and establish settlements and trade routes. As they discovered and conquered lands, they left a significant impact on the economy of a specific location.

Basically, the Vikings heavily influenced the economy during the Middle Ages, as they developed market towns and established currency systems or barter.

Religion

As depicted in the sagas and several historical accounts, the Vikings are highly religious people. They believed and worshipped in different gods and goddesses much like other great civilizations such as the Egyptians, Romans, Greeks, and Indians.

One popular influence that the Vikings had in our modern practice of religion, especially in Christianity is the Christmas Tree. Scholars believe that the practice of decorating a tree during the Yuletide season originated from the Viking tradition of the Yggdrasil or the sacred ash tree that holds the Nine Realms.

CONCLUSION

At this point, you should already have a good sense of Norse Mythology, especially the Vikings who believed in such rich and diverse religious and cultural practices.

Reading about Norse Mythology is important because it will help us understand the mindset of the Vikings and how they shaped our modern world.

The body of knowledge concerning the ancient religion of Scandinavians are mainly written during the Christian era, and so it represents only a small fraction of the diverse sagas, poems, and other texts from the actual practitioners of the Norse religion.

However, these bits of information are enough to stir our imagination on the diverse and vividness of the pagan beliefs and practices of the raiders from the North who had the guts and the glory to rule over Europe for centuries.

Their stories, and the characters they adore is now part of our world heritage and the opportunity to take a glimpse in the minds of these ancient peoples who lived many centuries before us is truly amazing.

The legends of the Norse Mythology convey meaning that could help us gain wisdom. These stories can inspire us and even teach us important life lessons. While the Norse religion has faded into history, it is still relevant today for those who seek learning from the ancients.

www.ingramcontent.com/pod-product-compliance
Ingram Content Group UK Ltd.
Pitfield, Milton Keynes, MK11 3LW, UK
UKHW021342161125

8998UKWH00019B/217

9 781922 346216